AΩ

FORGIVE OTHERS
We Pray, Pray, Pray Series

Written by: Carline Constant and Gregory Constant
Illustrated by: Leena Shariq

Subtitle: FORGIVE OTHERS

For information contact us online at: www.sprinklejoybooks.com

Summary:

FORGIVE OTHERS takes us on a spiritual journey with Caleb, his best friend, Omar, and Caleb's grandmother. During a game in gym class, Omar doesn't pick Caleb to be on his team and hurts Caleb's feelings. Grandma encourages Caleb to practice the value of forgiveness to strengthen his relationship with God. Can Caleb embrace this challenging journey and forgive his best friend?

Subjects:
CYAC: 1. Prayer Children's Christian Forgiveness Realistic Fiction Book. 2. Faith Based Grandparent Grandchildren's Book Religious Christianity Realistic Fiction Book. 3. Godly Morals & Values-Prayerbook Forgiveness Book. 4. Kids SEL-Forgiving Others-Picture Book. 5. Kids Spiritual Life Lessons-Christianity. 6. Raising Spiritual Kids-Praying Habits-Christian Picture Book. 7. Emotions-Feelings-Forgive Others- Kids-Grandparent Christian Message Book. 8. Pray With Hanna Grandma & Caleb Christian Series-With Christian-Activities. 9. Christian Message Picture Book. 10. African American Christian Family-Realistic Fiction.

Identifiers:
Paperback ISBN # 979-8-9897681-4-1
Hardcover ISBN # 979-8-9897681-5-8
ebook ISBN # 979-8-9897681-4-1

Library of Congress Control Number: 2024907939

All scripture quotations marked (GNT) are from the Good News Bible Translation in Today's English Version-Copyright © 1993 by American Bible Society. Used by permission.

Printed in the United States of America
LCCN Imprint: Sprinkle Joy Publishing, New York.

10 9 8 7 6 5 4 3 2 1
First Edition: April 2024

Semi Realistic Art Style
For Ages 5-12

Sprinkle Joy Publishing Books

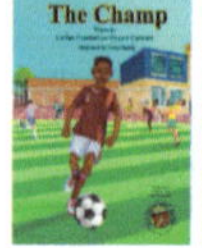  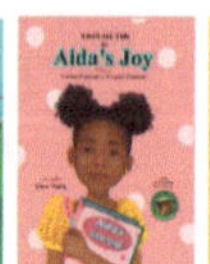    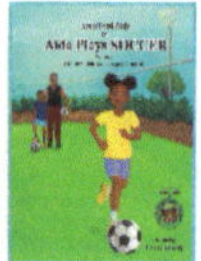  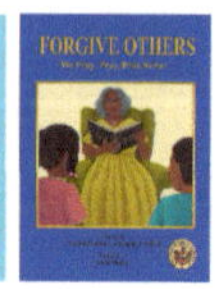

www.sprinklejoybooks.com

THIS BOOK
BELONGS TO:

____

WITH GRATEFUL HEARTS TO GOD!

To God be the glory!

****

This book is dedicated to my three sons, Gregory, Anthony, and Andy.

May God continue to mold and shape the three of you into responsible men.

Thanks to my family and friends for your words of encouragement.

Thanks to the editors for your contributions.

To all children and families worldwide.

-Carline Constant

Thanks to God for the many blessings.

-Gregory Constant

FORGIVE OTHERS

We Pray, Pray, Pray Series

Written by
Carline Constant and **Gregory Constant**

Sprinkle Joy
Publishing

My sister, Hanna, and I loved praying with Grandma.

GOD, THANK YOU FOR TODAY.
HOLY BIBLE

Sometimes, my friend, Omar, joined in our prayer routine.

"Children, God is loving, forgiving, and caring, always watching over us. God will put His angels in charge of us to protect us wherever we go," Grandma told us.

"Thank you, for a family that loves me and a friend who shares. God, thank you for my sister, she helps me with my homework," I prayed.

"God, thanks for protecting my family and the life you give us," Hanna added.

"God, thanks for my mother," said Omar. "She takes good care of me. Thanks for giving me fun friends to play with."

FREEZE!

After our prayers, Grandma took us to the park.

Omar and I loved to play freeze tag.

We ran, chased, tagged, froze, and unfroze.

It was so much fun.

"Caleb, you're my best pal!" Omar yelled.

"Way to go, Omar!" I cheered after he tagged me.

We created a "best buddy" handshake that only we

would know. I wished we could've kept playing,

but the sun was setting,

and it was time to go home.

"Thank God for my friend," I told Grandma.

"You and Omar make a great pair!"

Grandma laughed.

The next day at school, I couldn't wait for gym class.
It was the only class I had with Omar.
"Omar, you're freeze tag leader today," our gym
teacher announced. "Choose your team!"
Oh boy! Our favorite game! I couldn't wait to play!

Omar stood up, walked past me, and didn't
say a word. *Did he not see me?*
"Omar!" I waved at him, but he looked the
other way. One-by-one, Omar called out
names for his team...but he never called mine.
We had just played freeze tag at the park,
yesterday. He knew how good I was.

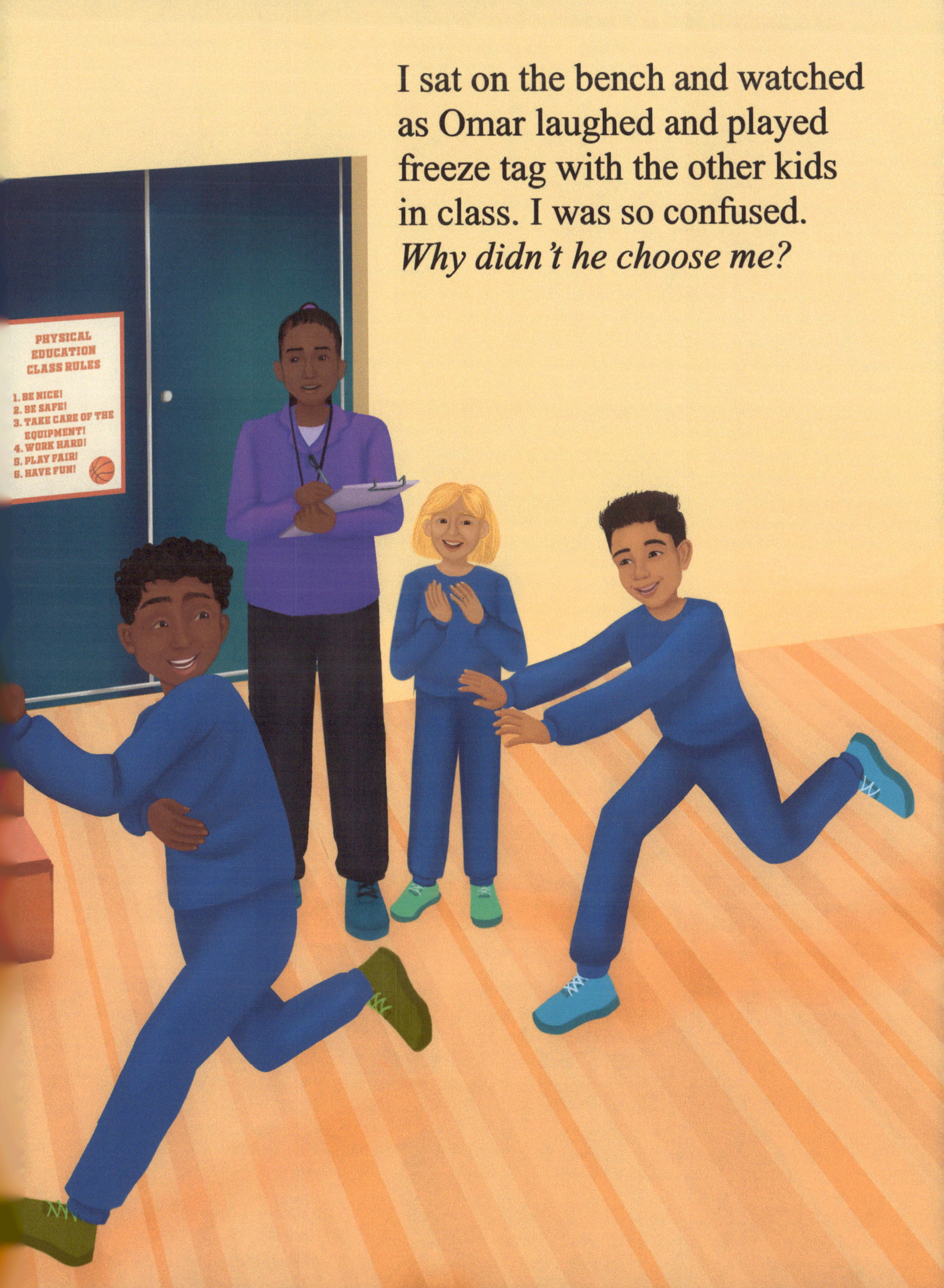

I sat on the bench and watched as Omar laughed and played freeze tag with the other kids in class. I was so confused. *Why didn't he choose me?*

Later that afternoon, Grandma picked us up from school. I was silent as we walked with Grandma.

Omar looked over at me. "Are you okay?"

"Why didn't you choose me in gym today?" I asked.

He shrugged. "Caleb, I didn't choose you to play freeze tag because we *always* play freeze tag. I wanted to give the other kids a chance to play."

So, he'd rather play with the other kids than me?

It's not fair. He still got to play.

Does he not like playing freeze tag with me

anymore? Is that it?

I turned away and didn't answer Omar.

His mother met us on our way home and left with

him before we reached the park.

When it's my turn to be freeze tag leader,

I won't choose Omar, I thought.

As Grandma and I reached the front of the house,

she asked, "Caleb, why are you so quiet?"

"Omar didn't choose me to play freeze tag at school

today," I told her.

"Oh, sweetie, I'm sorry to hear that.

I'm sure there's a good reason why.

Remember that people make mistakes sometimes

and God wants us to forgive each other," she said.

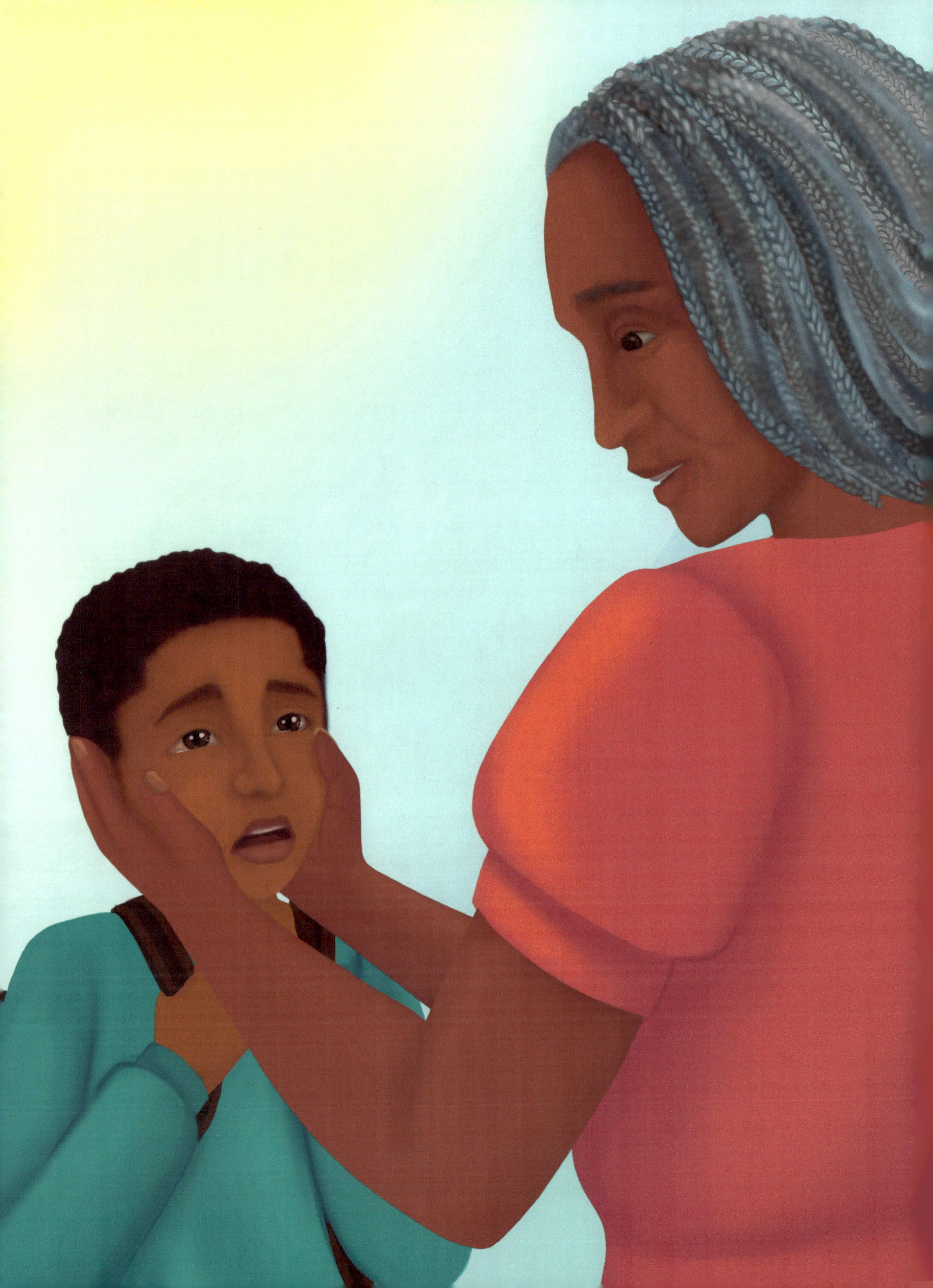

"The Bible says, 'If you forgive others
for the wrongs they've done to you,
your Father in heaven will also forgive you.'
Perhaps, you can find it in your heart to
forgive Omar," Grandma gently suggested,
holding my face in her soft hands.
"Forgive him *how*?" I mumbled.
"Be kind to Omar," Grandma replied.
"Come, let us go inside and pray."

I listened to Grandma's soft voice as she prayed,

"Thank you, God, for all that you do.

Forgive me, God, for my wrongs, and help me forgive others.

God, thank you for your love and forgiveness."

"Grandma, why does God need to forgive you?"

I asked.

"You're always helping people."

She smiled at me. "Caleb, our God is forgiving.

Sometimes people's actions and thoughts are

incorrect, no matter how much we help others."

Omar still should've chosen me, I thought.

"Grandma, it's not easy for me to forgive Omar,"

I mumbled.

"Caleb, when we forgive, we're able to let go of all

the hurt inside us and we don't stay upset,"

Grandma instructed.

"You know that God loves you

and you know that Omar cares about you.

We have faith in our God and must forgive one

another. I know you can get past this. Praise our

forgiving God for His blessings," Grandma

whispered.

That night, I thought, *Omar is my best friend. I don't think he was being mean when he didn't choose me. He did say he wanted to give the other kids a chance to play. I can forgive Omar.*

The next day, I waved at Omar when his mother dropped him off at my house.

Along with Grandma, we repeated our daily prayer.

"God will put His angels in charge of us to protect us wherever we go," we prayed with Grandma.

I silently prayed for God to help me set things right with my best friend and thanked God for giving me a good friend like Omar.

On the way to school, I turned to Omar.

"Hey Omar?" I started hesitantly.

"What is it?" Omar asked.

"I wanted to say I'm sorry for how I acted yesterday," I replied.

"Omar, it was nice of you to think about our classmates. I was sad that you didn't choose me to play the game, but I understand why you didn't. I was upset because I have fun playing with you and I felt left out."

"I'm sorry, Caleb." Omar frowned.

"I didn't mean to make you feel that way. Next time, I'll talk to you first."

We did our "best buddy" handshake and laughed.
As we reached next to the school,

I said in my heart, *God, thank you for your forgiveness and for guiding me on how to forgive others.*

Bible Verses:

"Forgive others, and God will forgive you."

(Luke 6:37 GNT)

"God will put his angels in charge of you to protect you wherever

you go."

(Psalms 91:11 GNT)

"Instead, be kind and tenderhearted to one another, and forgive

one another, as God has forgiven you through Christ."

(Ephesians 4:32 GNT)

"If you forgive others the wrongs, they have done to you, your

Father in heaven will also forgive you."

(Matthew 6:14 GNT)

"Forgive your brother or sister from your heart."

(Matthew 18:35 GNT)

"When you stand and pray, forgive anything you may have against

anyone, So that your Father in heaven will forgive the wrongs you

have done."

(Mark 11:25 GNT)

POSITIVE WORD SEARCH

Directions: Search for and circle the following words hidden in this puzzle.

EMOTIONS	FEELINGS	KINDNESS	TOGETHER
FORGIVENESS	FRIENDS	CHOICE	ACCEPTANCE
HOPE	GOD	~~PRAYER~~	

WHAT'S THE MAIN IDEA?

Directions: After reading, or listening to *FORGIVE OTHERS*, Describe the Main Idea of the story. Ask yourself, what is the story mostly about?" Give examples to support your answer.

MAIN IDEA:

SUPPORTING IDEA #1:

SUPPORTING IDEA #2:

SUPPORTING IDEA #3:

<u>**WORDS TO KNOW:**</u>

Bible: A collection of religious texts or scriptures that are sacred.

God: The creator of people and things.

Hope: To have faith, believe in God.

Prayer: Taking our thoughts to God and communicating with Him.

SEQUENCE OF EVENTS

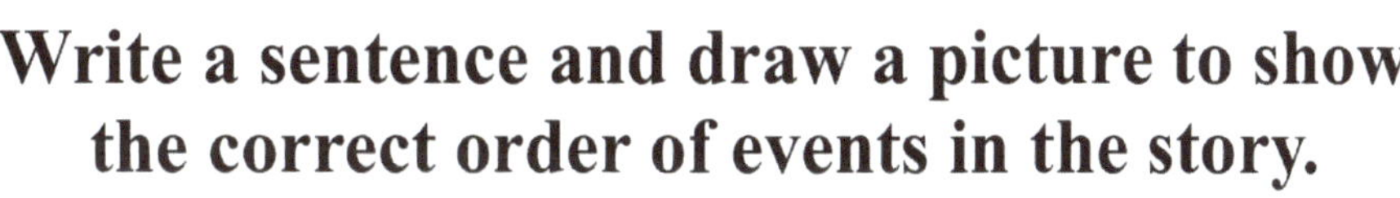

Write a sentence and draw a picture to show the correct order of events in the story.

Directions: After reading or listening to ***FORGIVE OTHERS***, complete the FORGIVENESS activity below.

↓Draw what happened.

	First __________________
	Next __________________
	Last __________________

WORDS TO KNOW:

Acceptance: To approve or take something giving to you.

Choice: To make decision between possibilities.

Forgiveness: Focus on positive thoughts to let go negative feelings.

Emotions: Changes your body goes through that sends impulses to your brain.

PRAYER CROSSWORD PUZZLE

Directions: Complete the crossword puzzle below.
Use the following words across or down.

| Acceptance | Choice | God | Friends | Feelings | Prayer |

| Forgiveness | Together | Hope | Kindness | Emotions |

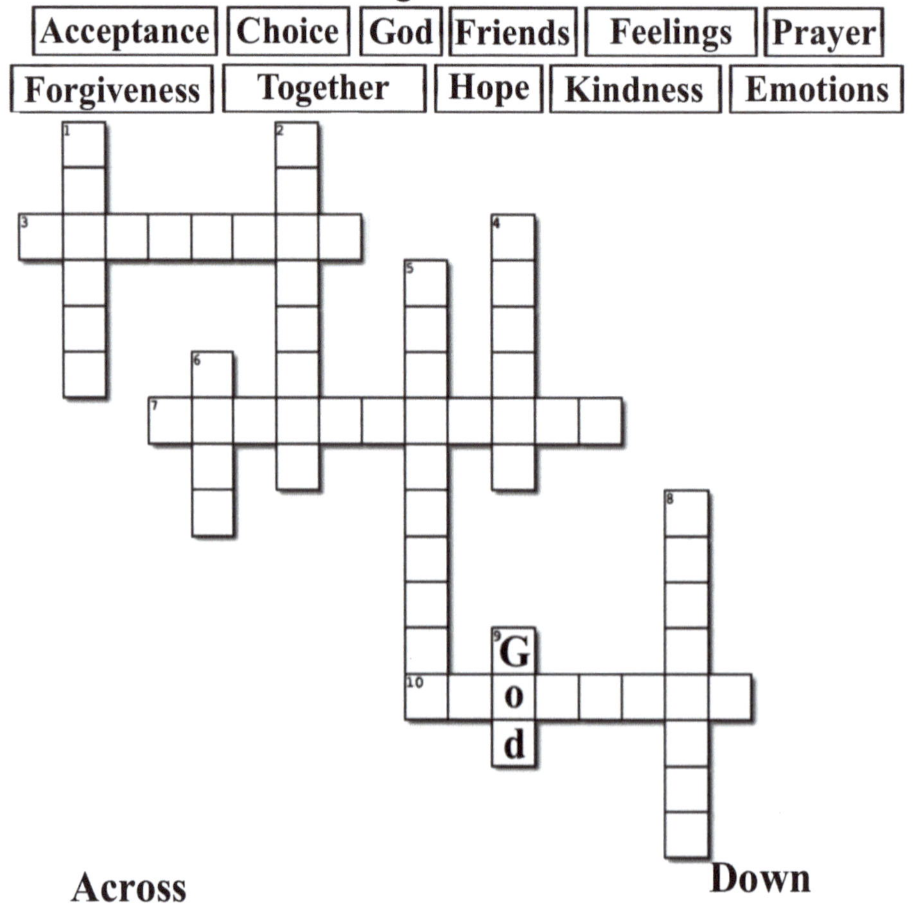

Across

3. ——————— we help and appreciate one another.

7. We focus on positive thoughts through ——————, letting of negative feelings.

10. —————— are changes in your body, such as happy, sad, that sets off impulses in your brain.

Down

1. Making a decision or taking a ______________ between possibilities.

2. A reaction that follows after an emotion ____________.

4. Through ____________ we take our thoughts to God.

5. To approve or take something giving to you is to make an ____________ .

6. To have faith is to have ____________ in God's blessings.

8. Helpful, caring friendship and charity are good deeds, important acts of

____________.

9. Our creator is ____ **God** ____ .

About the Authors:

Carline Constant and Gregory Constant are a mother and son duo dedicated to spreading positivity through literature. They hope Sprinkle Joy Publishing books touch the hearts and minds of people everywhere. Each sentence, illustration and story telling idea of Sprinkle Joy Publishing books are made with love!

Carline Constant is a mother, author, and educator. She earned a Master's Degree in Education from Brooklyn College City University of New York.

Gregory Constant is an author, entrepreneur, and technology professional. He earned a Bachelor's Degree in Informatics from the State University of New York at Albany.

For information about Sprinkle Joy Publishing Books contact us online at:
www.sprinklejoybooks.com

About the Illustrator:

Leena Shariq is a self-taught, Pakistan-based children's book Illustrator and Portrait Artist. Always encouraged by her parents, Leena started freelancing at the age of 16, and now, after only four years, she has illustrated many children's books, one after another.
Her body of work consists of semi realistic illustrations and stylised portraiture.

   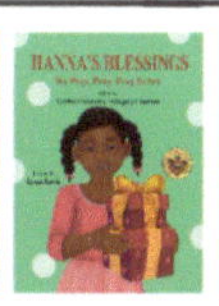 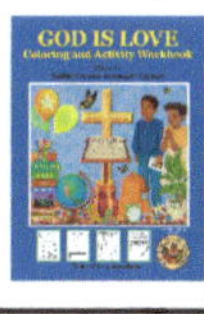       

(We Pray With Hanna, Grandma, & Caleb Series)
I AM THANKFUL
FORGIVE OTHERS
BE THANKFUL: Pray at Mealtime
Hanna's Blessings
GOD IS LOVE Coloring and Activity Workbook

Also, by Sprinkle Joy Publishing Books
(Aida and Amari Series):
The Champ
Amari and Aida SOCCER Coloring and Activity Workbook for Kids!
Aida's Joy
Aida's First Day of School.
Amari Plays Basketball.
Amari and Aida in HOW TO PLAY BASKETBALL.
Aida Plays SOCCER. (coming soon)
Amari's Helping Hands (coming soon)
Amari and Aida in FUN TIME Coloring & Activity WORKBOOK For Kids!
Thanks to God for ALL!

Thank you for your purchase!
Please leave an honest review. We read every review
and they help new readers discover our books.

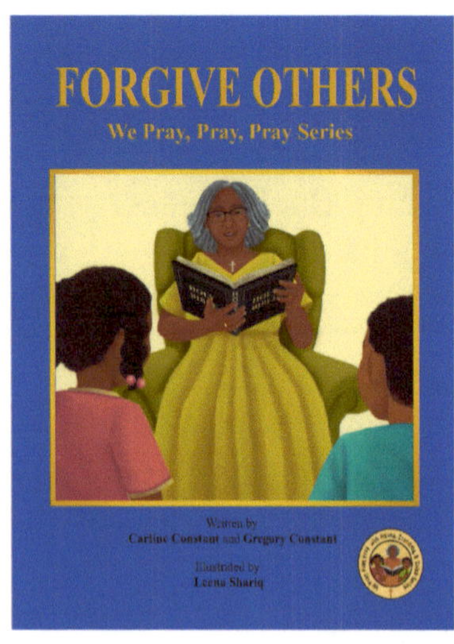

COMING SOON:
WE PRAY, PRAY, BE THANKFUL:
PRAY AT MEALTIME

Order Sprinkle Joy Publishing Books
www.sprinklejoybooks.com

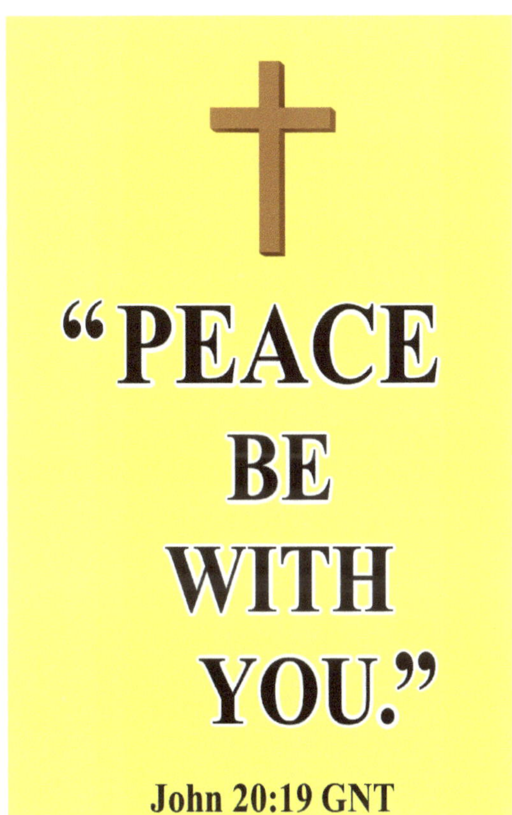

"PEACE
BE
WITH
YOU."
John 20:19 GNT

"Forgive others, and God will forgive you."
(Luke 6:37 GNT)

FORGIVE OTHERS takes us on a spiritual journey with Caleb, his best friend, Omar, and Caleb's grandmother. During a game in gym class, Omar doesn't pick Caleb to be on his team and hurts Caleb's feelings. Grandma encourages Caleb to practice the value of forgiveness to strengthen his relationship with God. Can Caleb embrace this challenging journey and forgive his best friend?

Sprinkle Joy
Publishing
www.sprinklejoybooks.com

I AM THANKFUL

We Pray, Pray, Pray Series

Written by

Carline Constant and **Gregory Constant**

Illustrated by

Leena Shariq